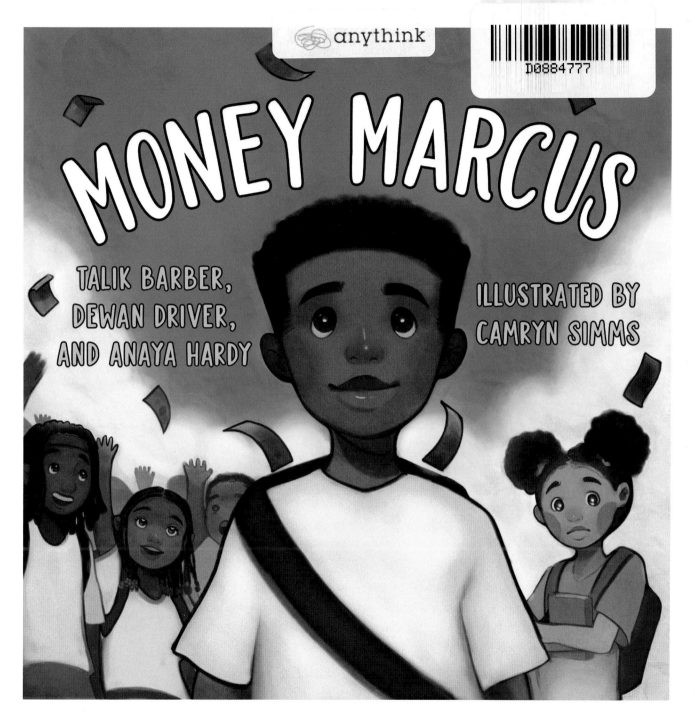

MONEY MARCUS

TALIK BARBER,
DEWAN DRIVER,
AND ANAYA HARDY

ILLUSTRATED BY
CAMRYN SIMMS

Reach Incorporated | Washington, DC

Shout Mouse Press

Reach Education, Inc. / Shout Mouse Press
Published by
Shout Mouse Press, Inc.

Shout Mouse Press is a nonprofit writing and publishing program dedicated to amplifying underheard voices. This book was produced through Shout Mouse workshops and in collaboration with Shout Mouse artists and editors.

Shout Mouse coaches writers from marginalized communities to tell their own stories in their own voices and, as published authors, to act as agents of change. In partnership with other nonprofit organizations serving communities in need, we are building a catalog of inclusive, mission-driven books that engage reluctant readers as well as open hearts and minds.

Learn more and see our full catalog at www.shoutmousepress.org.

Copyright © 2019 Reach Education, Inc.
ISBN-13: 978-1-950807-04-8 (Shout Mouse Press)

This book is dedicated to all the kids
who struggle to find a true friend.

Marcus wasn't the coolest kid at Reach Elementary School.

The other kids weren't very nice to him.

They made fun of his hand-me-down clothes and his raggedy backpack.

"Boy, you look like all your clothes come from the thrift store!"

"Look at his shoes! Them things messed up!"

The kids all laughed at him.

When the kids teased him, Marcus felt bad. He wished he had enough money to buy new stuff like they did. Maybe then he'd be popular.

But Marcus did have one real friend. Taylor was one of the cool kids, but she didn't care that Marcus wore old clothes or had no shoelaces. She just loved that they played video games together, danced, and sang karaoke!

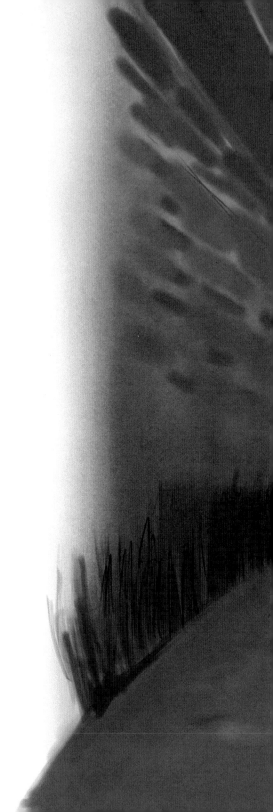

On the last day of school, Marcus was excited to leave the bullies behind. He was ready to spend all summer having fun with Taylor!

Marcus was cruising down the street on his way home when he found a piece of paper on the ground. He bent down to pick it up. Only it wasn't a piece of paper—it was a lottery ticket!

He looked around but he didn't see anyone who had dropped it.

The date on the ticket was today!

Marcus wondered, "Should I check the numbers?"

At home, all Marcus could think about was the ticket.

He tried to play Kidsnite online, but he couldn't focus.

He tried to watch videos on KidsTube, but everything bored him.

At dinner he scarfed down his food in a hurry so he could rush to the TV and find out if he won the lottery.

Finally, the numbers were called: 24, 35, 47, 38, 49.

The numbers on the screen matched the numbers on his ticket! Marcus won!

He was so happy he danced and then hit the woah.

Then he called his best friend Taylor. "Taylor guess what?! I won the lotto!"

"OMG! Are you serious? Are you capping?" said Taylor.

"Nah, I'm not bluffing! I really won!" said Marcus. "Meet me at the mall tomorrow and I'll show you!"

The next day, Marcus brought his backpack filled with money to the mall. He opened the backpack and showed it to Taylor.

"Wow, you really were telling the truth. What are you gonna do with all that money!?"

Marcus smiled. He knew exactly what he wanted to do. "Let's go to the arcade!"

Marcus and Taylor went to the arcade and played ALL the games.

Thanks to Marcus and the lottery money, they never ran out of coins. They had so many coins they had to put them in little money bags.

Across the game room, Kayvon from Mrs. Jones' class saw Marcus with the bags.

"Hey Marcus," he said, "how'd you get all those coins?"

"I won the lottery! We can play all the games we want now."

Kayvon grabbed his phone and took a picture of Marcus with the bags of coins.

He posted the photo on Kidstagram saying, "Yo! Marcus won the lottery!" #MoneyMarcus.

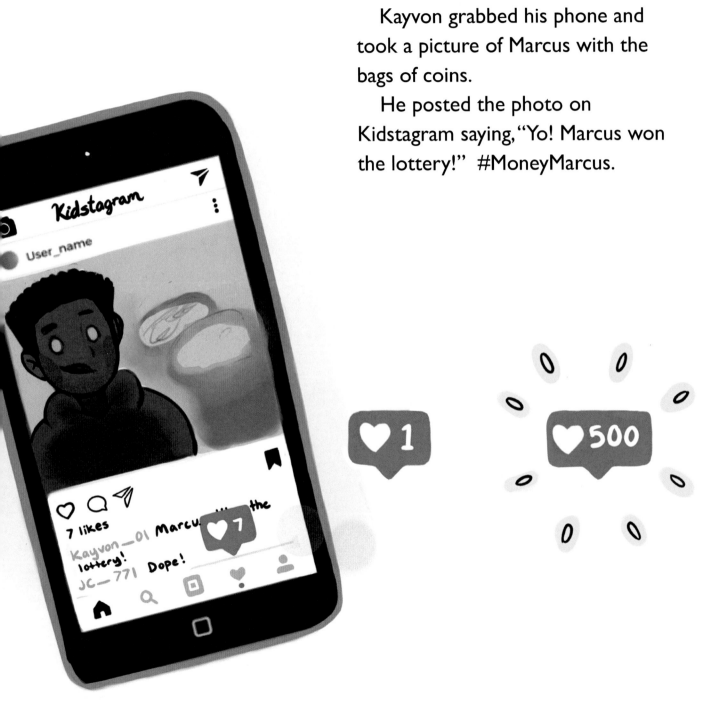

The post got one like. Then fifty likes. Then five hundred!
Soon it was the number one trending post on Kidstagram.
EVERYONE knew about Marcus winning the lottery.

Everyone who saw the post showed up to the arcade to play games with Marcus.

They shot hoops and raced cars. They did whack-a-mole and played pinball. They even played laser tag. They won so many tickets!

When they finished playing games, they went to the prize counter and got whatever they wanted. Marcus got a big teddy bear for Taylor and a PS4 for himself.

Marcus was smiling from ear to ear. He turned to his side to smile at Taylor, but the crowd of kids around him was too big! He couldn't see her at all.

Marcus started to look for her, but the other kids said, "Come on Marcus, let's go to the food court!" Marcus realized that after all that playing, he had worked up an appetite.

First, they went to Chipotle and ordered 18 burritos, 25 tacos, and 20 bowls.

The Kidstagram kids sat down by Marcus and ate it all, but they still wanted more.

"Hey Money Marc, since we're friends now can we order some more food?"

They went to Pizza Hut and ordered 15 large pepperoni pizzas. But even that was not enough.

"Can we also get dessert?" they asked.

Marcus almost never got dessert at home, so he said YES. Everyone followed him to Froyo. They ordered quadruple scoops with sprinkles, chocolate fudge, and caramel. All the good stuff.

Marcus had never felt so good. He didn't even care about how much money he was spending. He just liked all the attention he was getting from his new friends.

After lunch, Marcus and the Kidstagram kids walked around the mall.

"So Money Marc, what's up with your clothes, bruh?"

"You got money now so you gotta look sweet!"

In the mirror, Marcus looked at his reflection. His hoodie was faded and his shoes were dusty. Maybe they were right. Maybe he should change it up?

"Come on! Let's go shopping. We gotta style you."

Marcus followed the crowd to a store he'd never been to before. He went to the dressing room and waited behind the curtain while the other kids brought him piles of clothes to try on. They brought polo shirts, jackets, and designer jeans... and then they brought chains, shades, and flip flops, too. They gave him so many clothes, Marcus didn't know what to wear!

He came out of the dressing room rocking a new outfit: Gucci shirt, dark jeans, red bottoms. Marcus wasn't sure. The clothes weren't really his style but the kids seemed to like them. "How do I look?" he asked.

"Sweet!"

The Kidstagram kids kept bringing Marcus things to try on, but after a while they stopped. Instead, they wanted Marcus to buy them things.

"Hey Marcus, I'll be your friend forever if you buy me this t-shirt!"

"I'll be your friend if you buy me these jeans!"

Marcus felt frustrated. "I thought we were already friends?" He reached into his backpack and took out the money to buy the jeans, but he was feeling some type of way about it.

Then somebody else said, "We'll be best friends if you buy me these sunglasses!"

Marcus scrunched up his face in confusion. "What?!"

Marcus already had a best friend. He thought about Taylor, and how she always stood by him even before he found the lottery ticket. "You don't need nice things to make friends," she'd told him.

Enough was enough.

"Y'all all fakes!" Marcus shouted. "If you were really my friends you would've hung out with me before all this money."

Marcus gathered his shopping bags, threw on his backpack, and stormed away.

Marcus walked around the mall with his head down. He looked at his red bottoms. These shoes weren't even him. He was just wearing these clothes to look cool for the Kidstagram kids.

I miss Taylor, he thought.

He wished she was here with him. He had gotten so caught up with the Kidstagram kids that he forgot to look out for his best friend.

Marcus wandered away from the stores and past
the food court. When he looked up he was back at
the arcade. There was a girl sitting by the entrance
looking sad. But it wasn't just any girl. It was Taylor.

Marcus sat down beside Taylor. When she saw him, she crossed her arms and frowned. Her face looked like the angry emoji. Before Marucs could say anything, Taylor asked, "What are you wearing? You look corny."

"You're right."

"Also, you left me for those fake people. They treated you like trash in school and now they only like you for your money. I've been your friend since kindergarten."

"I know, but when they were all hanging around me, I felt popular. I felt like they really cared about me. But now I know that they don't."

"I understand. I'm still a little mad at you, though. You really hurt my feelings."

"That's fair. I'm sorry."

They sat together a moment in silence.

"So…" Taylor said. "You wanna go play Dance Dance Revolution?"

THE END

About the Authors

Anaya Hardy

is a fourteen-year-old sophomore at Ballou High School. Her hobbies include running track and being a part of JROTC. This is her first Reach children's book. She wrote this book to let kids know that money can be useful, but that true friendship is more important. It's good to have the right friendships around you and people who care.

Talik Barber

is a sixteen-year-old senior at Dunbar Senior High School. He enjoys spending time with his family and playing football and sometimes basketball. This is his second published children's book with Reach and Shout Mouse. He is also an author of *Tyrell's Big Move* (2018). He wanted to write this story because he has fun creating positive messages for children.

Dewan Driver

is a fifteen-year-old sophomore currently enrolled in Roosevelt High School. He likes playing basketball, listening to music, playing chess, and eating. This is his first Reach book. He wrote this story so he could help kids choose their friends.

Faith Campbell served as Story Coach for this book.

Hayes Davis served as Head Story Coach for this year's series.

About the Illustrator

Camryn Simms

is an illustrator pursuing a BFA in Communication Arts at Virginia Commonwealth University. Her love for comics and picture books growing up has led her to have a special place in her heart for visual storytelling. She is passionate about vivid artwork that engages the imagination. She enjoys working in a variety of different mediums, often finding that she has the most fun exploring the world of art. Ultimately, she hopes that readers can connect to her work and take something meaningful away with them.

Writers and artists at work

Acknowledgments

For the seventh summer in a row, teens from Reach Incorporated were issued a challenge: compose original children's books that will both educate and entertain young readers. Specifically, these teens were asked to create inclusive stories that reflect their lived experiences, so that every child has the opportunity to relate to characters on the page. And for the seventh summer in a row, these teens have demonstrated that they know their audience, they believe in their mission, and they take pride in the impact they can make on young lives.

Thirteen writers spent the month of July brainstorming ideas, generating potential plots, writing, revising, and providing critiques. Authoring quality books is challenging work, and these authors have our immense gratitude and respect: Jesse, Jailah, Victoria, Jocktavious, Talik, Anaya, Dewan, Riley, London, Shirelle, Camal, Japan, and Dameona.

These books represent an ongoing collaboration between Reach Incorporated and Shout Mouse Press, and we are grateful for the leadership provided by members of both teams. From Reach, Anika Rich contributed meaningfully to discussions and morale, and the Reach summer program leadership of Kim Davis and Jusna Perrin kept us organized and well-equipped. From the Shout Mouse Press team, we thank Head Story Coach Hayes Davis, who oversaw this year's workshops, and Story Coaches Barrett Smith, Marisa Kwaning, Faith Campbell, and Amy Sawyer for bringing both fun and insight to the project. We can't thank enough illustrators Camryn Simms, Anthony White, Joy Ingram, and India Valle for bringing these stories to life with their beautiful artwork. Finally, Amber Colleran brought a keen eye and important mentorship to the project as the series Art Director and book designer. We are grateful for the time and talents of these writers and artists!

Finally, we thank those of you who have purchased books and cheered on our authors. It is your support that makes it possible for these teen authors to engage and inspire young readers. We hope you smile as much while you read as these teens did while they wrote.

Mark Hecker
Reach Incorporated

Kathy Crutcher
Shout Mouse Press

About Reach Incorporated  Reach

Reach Incorporated develops readers and leaders by preparing teens to serve as tutors and role models for younger students, resulting in improved literacy outcomes for the teen tutors and their elementary school students.

Founded in 2009, Reach recruits high school students to be elementary school reading tutors. After completing a year in our program, teens gain access to additional leadership development opportunities, including The Summer Leadership Academy, The College Mentorship Program, and The Reach Fellowship. Through this comprehensive system of supports, teens are prepared to thrive in high school and beyond.

Through their work as reading tutors, our teens noticed that the books they read with their students did not always reflect their lived experiences. As always, we felt the best way we could address this issue was to put our teens in charge. Through our collaboration with Shout Mouse Press, these teens create engaging stories with diverse characters that invite young readers to explore the world through words.

By purchasing our books, you support student-led, community-driven efforts to improve educational outcomes in the District of Columbia.

Learn more at www.reachincorporated.org.